Richmond S. Dement

Field-Gar-A-Jim

Richmond S. Dement

Field-Gar-A-Jim

ISBN/EAN: 9783337402525

Printed in Europe, USA, Canada, Australia, Japan

Cover: Foto ©Andreas Hilbeck / pixelio.de

More available books at **www.hansebooks.com**

"I REGARD IT AS MY PLAIN DUTY TO SUSPEND YOU IN ORDER THAT THE OFFICE MAY BE HONESTLY ADMINISTERED"
R.B. HAYES.

"CREDIT MOBILIER" "DE GOLYER"

FIELD-GAR-A-JIM.   BIG-RO-GAR-THUR.

FIELD-GAR-A-JIM.

NOT

By H. W. L.

CHICAGO:
1880.
ORDERS SUPPLIED BY THE WESTERN NEWS CO.

PREFATORY REMARKS.

The author begs to state to his Republican readers (and, no doubt, admirers) that he has confined the first five chapters of this pamphlet wholly to facts elicited from Republican data, and should there, perchance, be found anything in those chapters which, seemingly, partakes of the nature of that, just at present, most undesirable amusement with Republicans, known by the popular phrase of "mud-slinging," it will, therefore, be understood that it is only Republican mud. The author further begs to express his regrets that, in sticking so close to the Republican records, and thereby meriting their choicest encomiums for his fidelity, he is compelled to use many words that are rather more expressive than elegant, or do violence to the authorities. He trusts that his frankness and great sincerity will be appreciated when he adds, that after it has conducted five successive campaigns so entirely upon the merits of opprobrious epithets (notably offensive) the Republican party suddenly offers a most refreshing study in its present virtuous amazement at anything of the kind, and a most interesting spectacle, surely, in its endeavor to pose as the sublimely respectable.

Finally, it is trusted that this little book will be received as an expression of the author's congratulations to Republicans upon the fact that, though on the very eve of their nominations their sun is setting (perhaps to rise no more forever), they may discover, through its last, lingering, *golden* rays, that "their chickens are coming home to roost."

We come! Why shrink? Canst not our presence brook?
Now we approach: so, if thou canst, remain!
—*Goethe's Faust, Part Second, Act V.*

What hands are here? Ha! they pluck out mine eyes!
Will all great Neptune's ocean wash this blood
Clean from my hands?
—*Macbeth, Act II, Scene II.*

"See, where his grace stands 'tween two clergymen!
*   *   *   *   *   *   *
And, see, a book of prayer in his hand,
True ornaments to know a holy man —"
*   *   *   *   *   *   *
"Cousin of Buckingham, and you sage, grave men,
Since you will buckle fortune on my back,
To bear her burthen, whether I will or no,
I must have patience to endure the load:
But if black scandal, or foul-faced reproach,
Attend the sequel of your imposition,
Your mere enforcement shall acquittance me
From all the impure blots and stains thereof;
For God he knows, and you may partly see,
How far I am from the desire thereof."
—*King Richard III, Act IV, Scene VII.*

FIELD-GAR-A-JIM.

Should you ask me, whence this jingle?
Whence the music of this measure,
With its tintinnabulations,
With its soft reverberations,
With its frequent repetitions?
I should answer, I should tell you,
Honor bright, "I know I stole it
From the Bard of Hiawatha."

Should you ask me, whence this story?
Whence this legend, this tradition,
With the odor of canal boats,
In their swish of dirty waters,
With the odor that's peculiar
To the swash of politicians,
With the dews and damps of Congress,
With the death damps of the nation?
I should answer, I should tell you,

"From the land of the Ohio,
From the land of office snatchers,
From the records made in Congress,
Where small politicians languish.
From the men who made the records,
Filed them in the nation's archives,
Nation with the very big N,
And the rickety foundation."

Ye who love truth for its own sake,
Love the truth without a thought for
Who it hits or who it misses,
Listen to this simple story.
Ye who love the fruits of office
Better than unsullied honor,
Step one side or stand from under.

CHAPTER I.

I.

Once upon a time (now listen),
In the land of the Ohio,
Land of mighty office-snatchers,
Where the muddy, nasty water
Floated "ager" and canal boats,
Where the Dusk-kwo-ne'she* flourished,
Where the Sugge-ma† are numerous,
Where the festive, gay Dahin-da‡
Sported in the emerald quagmire,
Was a mule, of sober visage,
Sober habits, and most sober,
Melancholy disposition.

II.

This sad mule had lost its rider,
Or was just about to lose him,
(Which is which it does not matter)

---

* Dusk-kwo-ne'she = Dragon flies.
† Sugge-ma = Mosquitos.
‡ Dahin-da = Bull-frogs.

And was just about to lose her
(Female mule) soft situation.

III.

Where the fields of corn were bending
With the weight of glowing harvests,
Where the clover fields and meadows
Reveled in the sun's warm kisses,
Freighting every passing zephyr
With the perfume of their gladness,
Sat upon the fence a young brave,
Whom the gods named Field-gar-a-jim,
Field-gar-a-jim, The-in-no'-cent.

IV.

What there is in a canal boat
Calculated to enrapture
All the senses, hold them spell-bound,
Never has been demonstrated.
But the fact is, as we find it,
Field-gar-a-jim was entranced
In the vision spread before him,
The, to him, most charming vision
Spread out on the dirty water.

V.

Lost, to him, the scene behind him;
Glowing harvests, clover blossoms,
Pleasant fields in dew drops bathing,
Pleasant fields in sunbeams basking,
Sunbeams sporting with the zephyrs
In the dew drops and the clover;
He had turned his back upon them.
On the fence was Field-gar-a-jim,
Field-gar-a-jim, The-in-no-cent,
On the fence that separated
Noble toil from degradation.

VI.

What there may be in the visage
Of a sober, melancholy,
Half starved mule that should inspire one
To political ambition,
Leave we for the philosophic.
We confine ourselves to facts, and
Figures, as you'll see directly.

VII.

Fact the first, then, Field-gar-a-jim.
Fact the second, he was honest,

That is, practically honest,
At this period of the story.
Fact the third, as has been stated,
Looked he on the mule with longing,
Longing that could not be uttered,
So you'll please excuse me from it.
Fact the fourth, we find him on it,
On the mule and on the tow-path,
On the road that lead to Congress.

VIII.

What there may be in a tow-path
That resembles the great highway
Leading to the halls of Congress,
Is, no doubt, at once suggested
In the fact that any mule, or
Any man, or any jackass,
May aspire to travel on it.

IX.

What there is, besides, suggestive
In the fact that he who travels
On this path must wear a harness,
Be he mule, or man, or jackass;
And what further is suggested

By the tow-line trailing after,
Through the nasty, dirty water,
Dragging its unseemly burden
Through the filth-begrim'ed water;
What there may be of suggestion
Touching ships of state, and so forth,
Dragged through mud and filth, and so forth.
Or whatever was suggested,
Still beyond our indications,
To the youthful Field-gar-a-jim.
Fact the fifth proves he was master,
Master of the situation.
Fact the fifth; the step was easy
From canal hand down to Congress.

CHAPTER II.

I.

Where the river, the Potomac,
Rushes down to hide in ocean,
Where the wavelets of the river
Speed away like birds affrighted
From the very wicked city,
Where no guilty man escapes
(Because no guilty man is captured)
Choosing to resign his office,
Where the pretty female clerks are
Thicker than the Okaha'wis,*
Field-gar-a-jim met in pow-wow
With the big chiefs of the nation.

II.

Soon he learned the trick of glory,
Soon he was a peer among them;
Peer was he of Cos-co-ron'-kling
(Ka-te-did-he), shot-gun-ha'-ter;

* Potomac herring.

14

Peer was he of Lon-a-jo'-gin,
Far-famed as "The-dir-ty-work-er";
Peer was he of Much-e-feather,
Maine's big Injun, also peer of
Little Kid-de, Pe-wee-u-gene.

III.

Friend was he of Chief U-lis-ses,
Mighty smoker, jail-de-liv-rer;
Friend was he of Sylph-ling-bab-cock,
Great pipe-filler of U-lis-ses;
Friend of both Cam-e'-rons, friend of
Me-dil-jo-sef, Wish-e-wash-e,
Friend of everybody — friend of
Ape-an-thro-po-mor-phus-wil-liams,
Lan-dau-wil-liams, "Old-cor-rup-tion."

IV.

Stride by stride he rose to place, and
Stride by stride rose he to power.
In the pow-wows of the nation
Field-gar-a-jim rose to power.

V.

As chief of appropriations,
Held the keys to what was pleasant

In the pow-wows of the nation—
Held the keys to every fraud that
Innocently could get through it.

VI.

Here, as chief of the committee,
Found he how to serve De-Gol-yer,
Chief of the big pavement swindle.
Here De-Gol-yer wooed and won him,
Made him pretty little presents
(Item, of five thousand dollars
For a brief that ne'er was written).

VII.

Here the guileless Field-gar-a-jim,
Prince of saintly peculators,
As the sly and silent partner
Of Boss Shepherd, Leet and Stocking,
Put their schemes through his committee.

VIII.

Here the guileless, speculating,
Enterprising Field-gar-a-jim
Took his stock of Cre-da-mo-bil,
Then with saintly, sacred sorrow,

And so forth, he "lied" about it.
"Lied" about it when they caught him —
So, at least, said his own people,
People, the intensely loyal,
Of the great Po-land Committee.

IX.

Stride by stride he rose to power,
Stride by stride rose Field-gar-a-jim,
Till, as "most successful scoundrel,"
(Pardon us the very harsh words!
'Tis a most unpleasant duty
Makes us quote his party organs —
Quote the strong words of their "back files,")
"Slyest," "Slickest," and "Sublimest
Scoundrel" of the scurvy Congress,
He was made the chief among them,
Given the supreme command, with
Power, absolute and kingly,
In all knavery politic
That should guide his party's future.
Then laid he THE SCHEME COLLOSSAL!
This is how he played it, listen!

X.

First he drew the Chief U-lis-ses
To his very loving bosom,
Swore eternal fealty to him —
Made a compact strong as words can —
Swore he would devote his life, and
All he had, to the advancement
Of his great friend, Chief U-lis-ses.
Next took he Chief Much-e-feather
To the same great loving heart, and
Swore to him eternal friendship —
Made a compact like unto the
Compact made with Chief U-lis-ses.
Then embraced he Chief Sher-man-john
In the same fond, loving arms, and
Swore to him upon his faith, in
Ultimate success, and so forth,
He'd work for him — John — and so forth,
Winked at John and clapped his shoulder,
Put his finger on his lips, and
Winked again most innocently.

XI.

"So far so good," Field-gar-a-jim
Quoth unto himself. "Now for it —
Now to get hold of the money."
Then, by virtue of his power,
Power absolute and kingly,
His prerogative unquestioned
In all knavery politic,
Summoned he into his presence
All the great thieves of his party,—
One by one they stood before him.

XII.

"Ri-chard-son," quoth Field-gar-a-jim,
"Ri-chard-son, great Meg-is-sog'-won,*
What's left from appropriations?"
Quoth Ri-chard-son, Meg-is-sog-won,
"Lacks a trifle of a billion."
Quoth the guileless Field-gar-a-jim,
"Bring it to me by to-morrow."

XIII.

Next appeared the Sneak-thief-bel-knap,
Better known as Wife-ac-cu-ser.

* Meg-is-sog'-won = Purse-bearer.

"How much," quoth Chief Field-gar-a-jim,
"Yet remains of all your stealings?"
Quoth the Wife-ac-cu-ser, "Only
Four millions five hundred thousand."
"Bring it to me by to-morrow,"
Smiling, added Field-gar-a-jim.

XIV.

Next the Skipper, Ro-be-son-fraud,
Put in his august appearance,
With his "savings" of eight millions.
Cress-well, Little-pec-u-la-tion,
Came next with his small two millions.
Next the courtly Big-ro-gar-thur,
With a paltry, bare one million.
This is all the rogue would give up.

XV.

Me-dil-jo-sef, Wish-e-wash-e,
Humbly bowed, next, in *the presence.*
"Me sick Injun — little money,"
Quoth the impecunious Josef,
"Me will put up one trade dollar."
"Keep it, keep it, Wish-e-wash-e,"

Smiling, answered Field-gar-a-jim,
"Keep your dollar, Me-dil-jo-sef."

XVI.

Next came New York's Fraud-ling-murphy,
With ten millions in his wampum.
Next, Dear-brother-in-law-ca-sey,
With his stealings of six millions.

XVII.

Smiled the saintly Field-gar-a-jim,
As his eye ran up the figures,
All the figures thus reported;
Smiled again as Sylph-ling-bab-cock
Brought in his reports from whisky.

XVIII.

"How much," quoth Chief Field-gar-a-jim,
"Has your noble band succeeded
In *reserving* from the whisky?"
Quoth the festive Sylph-ling-bab-cock,
"One billion five hundred millions."
"Bring it to me, here, to-morrow,"
Solemnly quoth Field-gar-a-jim.

XIX.

When he had cast up the column,
Happy was the guileless Chieftain.
"This," quoth he, with saintly smile,
"Is growing somewhat interesting—
This is comfortable, surely.
This, now, is a softer thing than
Riding lean mules on a tow-path—
Softer even this than preaching
To the mullet-headed Buckeyes."
Saying which he smiled serenely,
Oh, so guileless and so saintly!
Smiled as only that great smiler,
(Smiling Schuyler, once his partner
In the soft scheme Cre-da-mo-bil,)
Else beside him ever could smile.
In his hands was all the money,
Ergo in his hands all power.

CHAPTER III.

I.

Speed the years, the plot grows thicker.
Left, the bosom friend, U-lis-ses.
Left, the dear friend, Much-e-feather.
Left, the loving friend, Sher-man'-john.
Whoop-la! Whoop-la for Ru-ther'-ford!
(Oh, sly Jimmy, Field-gar-a-jim!
Guileless, saintly Field-gar-a-jim.)

II.

"Wheel in line, great Chief U-lis-ses,
Wheel in line, your turn shall come next!"
"Wheel in line, dear Much-e-feather,
Wheel in line, your turn shall come next!"
"Wheel in line, oh, fond Sher-man'-john,
Wheel in line, your turn shall come next!"
(Oh, sly Judas, Field-gar-a-jim,
Slyest, slickest, saintliest sinner.)

III.

Oh, the canvas! Oh, the people!
Oh, the speeches! Whoop-la! Whoop-la!
Oh, the bloody shirt, and so forth!

IV.

Oh, the wailing of the chieftains!
Oh, the cursing, swearing, raving!
Ru-ther-ford-be is defeated!

V.

From the dust and smoke of battle,
From defeat and from disaster,
From the swearing and confusion,
Rose the form of Field-gar-a-jim,
With an innocent, sweet smile and,
In his eye, a brilliant "i-dee."

VI.

Speed the days, the plot is thick'ning —
Whoop-la! Whoop-la! Liz-zie-pinc-ston!
Whoop-la! "the returning boards" and
Whoop-la! visitors, the statesmen!
Whoop-la! Whoop-la, Field-gar-a-jim,
Chief of visitors, the statesmen!

VII.

Speed the days, the plot grows thicker.
Whoop-la! Whoop-la, Eight to Seven!
Whoop-la! Whoop-la, Field-gar-a-jim,
Big Chief of the Eight to Seven!

VIII.

Speed the hours, the plot grows thicker —
Thicker — thicker — it is solid!
Solid are the eight, and solid
Ru-ther-ford-be with the nation —
Nation with a very big N
And most rickety foundation.
Whoop-la! Whoop-la, Field-gar-a-jim!
"Slickest," "slyest" and "sublimest
Scoundrel" of the scurvy Congress

CHAPTER IV.

I.

Speed the years, the *Seheme Collossal*
Grows apace. U-lis-ses wanders
Over seas in search of buncomb,
Drawing on the Fund-Corruption,—
Field-gar-a-jim's Fund-Corruption.
Oh sly, slick and slippery Jimmy!
Oh in-no-cent Field-gar-a-jim!
Much-e-feather must be slaughtered.

II.

Speed the years, the *Scheme Collossal*
Rapidly tends toward solution.
Lo, the wigwam! Lo, the pow-wow!
Lo, the chieftains of the pow-wow!

III.

Cos-co-ron-kling, (Ka-te-did-he),
Champion of Chief U-lis-ses!
Lon-a-jo-gin, dir-ty-work-er,

Second of Chief Cos-co-ron-kling,
In all matters tending Grant-ward!

IV.

Brass-tongue-frye-frye, Champion of
Main's big Injun, Much-e-feather!
Pe-wee-u-gene, very-lit-tle,
Second of Chief Brass-tongue-frye-frye.

V.

Lo, the cats of famed Kilkenny!
Lo, the coming match between the
Champions of Chief U-lis-ses
And of Great Chief Much-e-feather!

VI.

Lo! the sly, slick, slippery Jimmy,
Champion of Chief Sher-man'-john!

VII.

Lo, the solitary Granger,
Champion of Field-gar-a-jim!
Oh, sly, slick and slippery Jimmy!
Oh, my eye, oh, how he played it!
Oh, the guileless Field-gar-a-jim!
Lo, the solitary voter!

VIII.

Lo, the two Kilkenny cats, and
Lo, the bland and child-like face of
Field-gar-a-jim, The-in-no'-cent!
Oh, my eye, now here was richness!

IX.

Eloquent was Cos-co-ron-kling,
Sweet his tones and soft his accents
Even as when Ka-te-did-he.

X.

Eloquent was Lon-a-jo-gin,—
Eloquent as when he mustered
Soldiers for the Rebel army.

XI.

Eloquent was Brass-tongue-frye-frye—
Rang his tones out in the wigwam,
Musical as any jackass.

XII.

Even eloquent was Pe-wee,—
Very little, Pe-wee-u-gene.

XIII.

But oh, sweet as the Æolian,
Sweet as honey in the comb, or

Out of it, spread on hot buckwheats,
Was the sweet and saintly voice, and
Was the sweeter, saintlier smile of
Field-gar-a-jim, The-in-no-cent!
Friend was he of everybody.

XIV.

In-ger-sol-bob from the platform
Stole out like Longfellow's Arab,
Went around behind the wigwam,
Damned all preachers, chewed tobacco.

XV.

Many chiefs whom we might mention
(But we shall not—don't be frightened)
Having seats in the Convention
Aired their eloquence, and so forth,—
Fouled the fouler air, and so forth,—
With their foulest breaths, and so forth.

XVI.

Speed the show, bring out the tumblers!
Oh, the high and lofty tumbling!
Speed the show! the sport increases—
Oh, the elephant and monkey!

Oh, the clown! and oh, the donkey!
Oh, the two Kilkenny cats! and
Oh, the two cats raking chestnuts
For the gentle, guileless monkey!

XVII.

Eloquent is Cos-co-ron-kling,
But his smile grows very bitter,
And his words incline to wither,
And his voice is somewhat raspish.
The Adonis of the forum
Seems beset by strange emotions,
As when Katy's ancient landlord
Leveled on him with a shot gun.

XVIII.

Eloquent, still, Lon-a-jo-gin —
But that strange, peculiar kind of
Eloquence when bluff and bluster,
Arrogance and low buffoonery
Falls short of appreciation.
Lon-a-jo-gin's dirty work was
Too foul even for that Pow-wow.

XIX.

Taunting was the Brass-tongued-frye-frye,
Waspish, stinging, very bitter.
Taunting, too, was Per-wee-u-gene
Keeping pace with his quick leader.

XX.

But, oh sight for gods and men, and
Sight for women, for that matter,
(If Adonis-Ros-Coe were not
Posturing just at the moment)
Was the guileless Field-gar-a-jim!
Calm was he as any oyster.
Meek and gentle was his face, and
Low and soft his gentle accents.
Never was a sucking dove (If
Doves do suck — I've heard it doubted)
More innocent, inoffensive,
Humble, yielding, soft persuading,
Artless, altogether lovely.

XXI.

Speed the ballots, speeds the buncomb,
Speed the bosses of the ballots,
Speed the bosses of the buncomb.

XXII.

Much-e hot-e grow the chieftains
As the red hot day advances—
Hot as Hottentots and hotter,
Hot as Harriet Beecher's temper,
Hot as Pope Bob, cursing preachers,
Hot as Hell-e-nis-tic fire!

XXIII.

Still, amidst the general rumpus,
Placid, patient as his master,
Perfectly serene and conscious,
Lo! the solid, single voter!

XXIV.

Speed the ballots, speeds the buncomb,
Speed the bosses of the ballots,
Speed the bosses of the buncomb.

XXV.

Lo, the patient Field-gar-a-jim!
Lo, the guileless Field-gar-a-jim!
Lo, the saintly Field-gar-a-jim!
Lo, the solitary, solid,
Single vote for Field-gar-a-jim.

XXVI.

Break the ranks! Confusion's rampant!
Break the ranks! All hell can't stop it!

XXVII.

Hast thou seen the pent up waters,
Mighty waters, many fathoms
Deep and many fathoms broader,
Trickling through a tiny crevice,
Through the dam that barred their progress,
Through a single, tiny crevice?
Lo, the one vote! Lo, the crevice.

XXVIII.

Hast thou seen the mighty waters
Burst the levee, spread destruction?
Hast thou heard the rush of waters
Crashing, screaming, hissing, roaring?
Lo, the pow-wow in confusion!

XXIX.

Hast beheld a flock of sheep, and
Hast observed the tinkle, tinkle,
Of the bell on the one wether?
Lo, the granger! Lo the wether!

XXX.

Hast beheld the guileless shepherd
Drop a rider from the fence, and
Gently signal the said wether?
Lo, the shepherd, Field-gar-a-jim!

XXXI.

Hast beheld the wether jump it,
Jump the fence where it was lowest?
Hast beheld the sheep all follow?
Lo! the chieftains of the pow-wow!

XXXII.

Whoop-la! Whoop-la, Field-gar-a-jim!
Whoop-la! Whoop-la, Scheme Collossal.

CHAPTER V.

I.

Sing the wrath of Chief U-lis-ses.
Sing the woe of Sylph-ling-bab-cock.
Sing the grief of Cos-co-ron-kling —
Katy gone, too! Oh, Muse! Too much.

II.

Oh, the curses! Lon-a-jo-gin
Swore until he burst his wam-pum.
Cam-e-ron-don, son of Simon,
Swore till he ran out of words, and
Begged Pope Bob to lend him utterance.

III.

Oh, the ire of Much-e-feather
When he saw how they had played him!
Oh, the hot breath of Sher-man'-john!
Never was such cursing, swearing
Never was such raving, gnashing
Of false teeth twixt oaths, and so forth.

IV.

Oh, the wailing of the people,
Of the honest, sober people,
Of the yeomen of the party!
Ah! too well knew they the records,
Records laid up in the archives,
In the archives of the Nation —
Nation with the very big N
And the rickety foundation.

V.

They had read in their own journals,
The best journals of the party,
(More than a full hundred of them),
Of the records in the archives —
Records made by their own party.
(Once more pardon us these harsh words —
Frightful, but we cannot help it.
Though to us it is most painful,
We're compelled to quote the records.)
Records branding Field-gar-a-jim
As "a trickster very cunning,"
As "a base ring politician,"

As "a tool of every steal that
Rings and lobbies put through Congress,
As " a cringing, crawling coward,
Slinking from the field of battle,
Hiding in the halls of Congress,"
As "a smiling hypocrite," and
As "a thief," and as "a liar."
They had looked on Tom Nast's cartoons,
Cartoons of the Cre-da-mo-bil,
Cartoons branding Field-gar-a-jim
As "a hypocrite and liar."

VI.

They had had the proofs submitted
In these same best party journals,
Proofs sustaining all these charges,
Proofs they could not call in question.
And the *people* of the party,
They, themselves, in private, public,
Had been loud in their hot curses,
They could not blot out these records,
They could not recall their curses·
Records damning Field-gar-a-jim,

Curses damning Field-gar-a-jim.
Oh, the records! Oh, the records!*

VII.

Well they knew the Bourbons (d—n 'em)
Would call up the blighting record.
Well they knew the honest people,
Honest people of all parties,
Would not vote for Field-gar-a-jim.

VIII.

Oh, the record! Oh, the record!
The black record of their chieftain!
All the water of both oceans
Could not wash out that black record —
Rather would it foul both oceans.

IX.

Sing the fury of the chieftains
When they'd had time to consider —
Realize the scheme colossal —
Realize how their own savings,
Through Boss Shepherd, Leet and Stocking,
Through the slick De Golyer swindle,

* See Appendix.

Through the big steal, Cre-da-mo-bil.
Through over-appropriations,
Through Ri-chard-son, Megissog'won,
Through The-wife-ac-cu-ser-bel-knap,
Through the skipper, Ro-be-son-fraud,
Through Small-pec-u-la-tion-cress-well,
Through The-kite-tail-big-ro-gar-thur,
(Not to mention the trade dollar
Tendered to the general fund by
Me-dil-jo-sef, Wish-e-wash-e),
Through the customs frauds of Mur-phy,
Through the Broth-er-in-law-ca-sey,
Through the Sylph, sweet-scent-ed-bab-cock,
And through that great Non-de-script-us,
Ape-an-thro-po-mor-phus-wil-liams.
Realized how these "great savings,"
Savings for the fund cor-rup-tion,
Had been utilized against them.
When they realized still further
That the balance of the fund would
Still be utilized against them,
Utilized for Field-gar-a-jim —

Sing, oh naughty Muse, the raving.
Sing the wild despair and raving,
When was realized the length of—
Realized the depth and breadth of,
Field-gar-a-jim's *Scheme Collossal!*
Can't? Then sing of Field-gar-a-jim.

X.

Lo, the placid Field-gar-a-jim!
Lo, the guileless Field-gar-a-jim!
Saintly in his smile, and saintly
His soft tones and gentle accents.

XI.

"Wheel in line, oh, noble chieftains—
Wheel in line—your turns shall come next."

XII.

Quoth Achilles, Cos-co-ron-kling,
Sulking in his tent and brooding
On the loss of his Bri-se-is,
"Field-gar-a-jim, see you d—d first."

XIII.

Quoth great Hector, Don-cam-e-ron,
"Think I'd rather go a-fishing."

XIV.

Quoth U-lis-ses not a word, but
Silently smoked his Ha-va-na.

XV.

Lon-a-jo-gin, dir-ty-work-er
(Ready for the nastiest job that
Ever fell to man or beast, or
Any creeping, crawling thing), was
First to wheel in line of muster.
Quoth the slimy Lon-a-jo-gin,
"Here am I, great Field-gar-a-jim,
Son of Illinois, and so forth,
Far-famed for my deeds, and so forth,
Gory damns and smut, and so forth,—
Guess I'm just your man, and so forth."

XVI.

"Let us pray!" quoth Field-gar-a-jim.

A combination and a form indeed,
Where every god did seem to set his seal
To give the world assurance of a man.

—Hamlet.

CHAPTER VI.

I.

Where the waves of the Atlantic
Bear Aurora's first warm kisses
To the white sands and the brown clifts
Of Columbia's eastern border —
From the tribes of the Atlantic
Rose the cry, "Givé us a leader!"

II.

Where the waves of the Pacific
Kiss their hands back in the sunset
To the golden gates of plenty
Of America's rich treasures —
From the tribes of the Pacific
Rose the cry, "Give us a leader!"

III.

Where the lakes that belt the Northland,
Laughing in the glow of sunlight,
Dancing in the twinkling starlight,
Speed our commerce to all nations —

From the tribes of the great lakes there
Rose the cry, "Give us a leader!"

IV.

Where the orange groves are blooming,
Where the glory of the seasons
Dwells in groves of the magnolia,
In the cotton fields and rice fields,
From the tribes of valorous Southrons
Rose the cry, "Give us a leader!"

V.

Where the mighty Mississippi
Rolls in splendor to the ocean —
Where its tributary rivers
Frolic in the lap of plenty,
From the tribes where men are giants
Rose the cry, "Give us a leader!"

VI.

Rolled the echo through the mountains,
Rolled the echo through the valleys,
Till its loud reverberation
Called the people, as by magic,
To a council of the nation.

VII.

Where the city, Cincinnati,
Basks in regal, sunlight splendor,
Shut out from the world surrounding
By its hills of wondrous beauty,
Amphitheater more grand than
Elsewhere 'neath the dome of heaven,
Met the tribes in mighty council.

VIII.

Silently they journeyed thither,
From the Northland, from the Southland,
From the Eastland, from the Westland,
Silent, and with mighty tread, as
When an army moves to battle —
Silent, and with steady mien, as
When the crisis is upon them.

IX.

As the first faint tint of morning
Decked the orient with silver,
On the hilltops round the city
Stood the stately, silent thousands —
Every tribe had sent its wise men,
Many tribes had sent their warriors.

X.

Here was met nor clan nor faction;
Here was found nor strife nor discord;
But one voice was to be heard now;
But one spirit moved the people:
'Twas the Genius of Republics,
'Twas the Majesty of Tribes, that
Rose to save a falling nation.

XI.

As the day-god's glimmering lances
Shot above the gray horizon,
From the hilltops moved the people
Down the hillsides grandly silent,
Down into the quiet city.
Stately was their tread, and stately
Was the firm look on their faces.

XII.

Ere was reached the ample forum,
Halted were the countless thousands—
There was not space for the people,
Pressed within the circling hill-sides,
Filling all the spacious valley,—

Amphitheater whose dome was
The bright morning sunlit heavens.

XIII.

When to Manito the mighty,
Gitche-Manito the mighty,
They had offered their petitions,
Bowed their heads and asked His guidance
Then had come the great, auspicious
Moment that each tribe should be heard-
When each member of each tribe should
Name the one he'd have for leader.
'Twas for this they'd come together,—
That all tribes had met together
In a council of the nation,—
Trusting that in this great hour
Gitche-Manito the mighty
Would direct them and speak to them.

XIV.

Now was come the awful moment!
Sat the tribes with heads uncovered.
Awful was the silence, awful!
In the presence of Manito.

XV.

Rose the Council in a body,—
Rose the Council as by magic,—
On each face was written "vict'ry!"
From the throng went up a shout
That shook the great hills to their bases:
"Hancock! Hancock! Hancock! Hancock!"

XVI.

And the people from the hill tops
Took the shout up from the Council:
"Hancock! Hancock! Hancock! Hancock!"

XVII.

And the people in the valleys
Heard the shout rise from the hill tops,
And they shouted to the mountains,
"Hancock! Hancock! Hancock! Hancock!"

XVIII.

And the mountains sent the echo
Ringing back upon the valleys,
"Hancock! Hancock! Hancock! Hancock!"

XIX.

Till the nation rose together,
Shook the continent beneath them,
Shook the very dome above them,
With the shout of "Hancock! Hancock!"

XX.

And the superb, gallant soldier,
Proved on many a field of battle,
Idol of the grand old army,
Honored even by his great foes,
Shall be made chief of the nation.

XXI.

And the statesman of the crisis,
Crisis long to be remembered,
Shall defend our Constitution.

XXII.

And his name shall be "Defender
Of the grand old Constitution."

APPENDIX.

THE GREAT STEALS.

The amounts accredited in the foregoing pages to the peculations of the different members of General Grant's cabinet, and his favorites in power outside of the cabinet, are substantially correct. Of course we have been compelled to leave out very many names in the great catalogue of criminals that made up this administration of infamy. We have confined our lines to the names only of the most conspicuous.

THE COUNTING-IN FRAUD.

We have omitted the interesting history of the great " counting-in " fraud except in the few lines presented, and we take occasion to mention here that of the one hundred and three who participated in that world-renowned outrage, *one hundred and three* have been placed in remunerative offices by the present administration, notwithstanding the fact that the infamy of many of these was publicly confessed previous to their appointments.

51

CREDIT MOBILIER — THE POLAND REPORT.

The following are certified extracts from the report of the Poland Committee. It will be remembered that this Committee, appointed by Congress to investigate the Credit Mobilier transactions, was composed of five members, three of whom — Poland, Banks and McCrary — being exceedingly stauch republicans. We first quote from the sworn testimony of Mr. Garfield on the 14th of February, 1873. This was before he knew the character of the evidence against him:

"I state explicitly that no one ever gave, or offered to give, me any shares of stock in the Credit Mobilier or Union Pacific Railroad. I have never received nor had tendered to me any dividends, in cash, stock or bonds, accruing upon any stock in either of said organizations. I never received a dollar in bonds, stocks or dividends."

It is impossible to give here all of the evidence — it was quite voluminous — but we submit the "finding" of the Committee, so far as related to Mr. Garfield, the 18th of February, 1873:

"The facts in regard to Gen. Garfield, as found by the Committee, are that he (Garfield) agreed with Mr. Ames to take ten shares of Credit Mobilier stock, but did not pay for the same. Mr. Ames received the 80 per cent dividends in bonds, and sold them for 97 per cent, and also received the 60 per cent cash dividend, which, together with the price of the stock, and interest, left a balance of $329. This sum was paid over to Mr. Garfield by a check on the sergeant-at-arms, and *Mr. Garfield then understood this sum was the balance of dividends after paying for the stock.*"

In 1872 Mr. Garfield was elected to Congress by 11,000 majority. In 1874, the Credit Mobilier having occurred meantime, that majority was reduced to 2,528.

In 1876 the independent republicans proclaimed, in a set of resolutions passed in convention, "that there is no man to-day officially connected with the administration of our national government against whom are *justly* preferred *more* and *graver* charges of corruption than are *publicly made* and *abundantly sustained* against James A. Garfield, the present representative of this congressional district, and the nominee of the republican convention for reëlection. *That since he first entered Congress to this day there is scarcely an instance in which rings and monopolies have been arrayed against the interests of the people that he has been found in speech or vote upon the side of the latter, but in almost every case he has been the ready champion of the rings and monopolies.*"

The above is not italicized, of course, in the original document, otherwise the words are precisely as they appeared in the resolutions of the republican convention.

THE REPUBLICAN PRESS.

Of course, it would be impossible, in this little
book, to make extended quotations from the republican press of 1873, in which there was such pro-
nounced condemnation of Mr. Garfield's complica-
tions in the Credit Mobilier business. Every one
who is at all familiar with the political situation
at that time will remember that (to use military
terms) the fire was opened quite briskly along the
line and was sustained with remarkable energy.

The sublime and saintly composure of Mr. Garfield during this trying ordeal was the occasion of
grave fears on the part of his nearer friends that
he had lost his reason. His heroic cheek did not
blanch in the presence of the most indubitable
evidence of his knavery. *He knew too well that
the party could not afford to sacrifice him.*

The following extract from the Chicago *Times,*
pronouncedly independent, in which it quotes from
the Cincinnati *Commercial* of March 31, 1873, is all
we have room for here:

"It is the ammunition furnished by the republican journals themselves that is being used against
Gen. Garfield, and it is a little curious that those
now warmest in his defense, and least tolerant of
any inquiry into his record, were then most pro-
nounced in their charges. Thus the Cincinnati
Commercial, under date of March 31, 1873. Speak-
ing of Garfield under fire, it says:

'And Garfield's noble soul was sadly perturbed. He looked upon the scenes with grave apprehensions, and regarded this unseemly persecution of the righteous with such horror that his soul was sick within him. He came near making a fatal blunder once. After Ames had testified the second time as to the guilt of Garfield, *fixing it upon him clearly and unmistakably*, the General at once notified them that he would come before them and refute the vile slanders that the mendacious man from Massachusetts had poured out upon him. The day and the hour came, but simultaneously came not Garfield. He had heard that Ames (who was then reluctantly producing the receipts that Patterson had signed) had in his possession other such documents to prove the correctness of his testimony in respect to others, and the gallant General, whose flashing blade was wont to gleam adown the line in the gory days of the past decade, found that to stay away was prudent, and he never appeared. The complacent Committee forebore to question Ames further as to Garfield's statement and his own, and the papers were consequently never produced.'

So long as the files of leading republican journals contain matter of this kind, it will be idle upon the part of the Garfield press to frown down all mention of his alleged delinquencies."

THE DE GOLYER BUSINESS.

For the brief but exhaustive treatment of the De Golyer business in the following editorial, we

are again indebted to *The Times.* The entirely independent position of *The Times,* and as a conse-
quence, its proverbial accuracy in matters of political
data, gives what is submitted here a weight of
authority immeasurably beyond anything of the kind
that could be offered by a partizan.

"When the facts are so plain in the matter of
Garfield's fee, paid him by Dick Parsons for services
in procuring pavement contracts for De Golyer &
McClelland from the District of Columbia, it is
marvelous that there should continue to be such
wild asseveration on the one hand and such ignorant
denial on the other. The whole matter is of record,
first through a congressional investigation, next
in the circuit court of Cook county. Mr. Garfield
admits the receipt of a fee of $5,000, which was
placed to his credit in bank by Dick Parsons, who
had been employed by Chittenden to procure pavement contracts for the firm named. Mr. Garfield
claimed that the fee was for his service as a lawyer,
and that such service consisted in the preparation
of a laborious brief and the making of an argument
in favor of the particular kind of pavement which
De Golyer & McClelland desired to lay down — a
pavement, by the way. now abandoned as wholly
worthless. On cross-examination by Nickerson,
who was the owner of the 'ironized process,' the
same used in the pavement mentioned, General
Garfield admitted that he never filed a brief with
the Board of Public Works of the District of Columbia, and made no argument before the board.

He met Shepherd, and told him his opinion of the process. As the brief was never filed, and never published, there is a strong presumption that it was never prepared. For such service as he performed Mr. Garfield received $5,000. equivalent to the salary for a year as congressman. Chittenden claimed that the service of Garfield was worth the money paid him, since he was chairman of the committee on appropriations, the same from which Mr. Shepherd and the Washington ring must receive their favors. McClelland & De Golyer got their contracts. Chittenden claimed an interest in the profits, but his claim was not admitted by the firm; whereupon he commenced suit against them. The New York *Tribune* gives a statement of this case:

'Chittenden sued McClelland & Jenkins (formerly McClelland & De Golyer) upon a contract by which they agreed to pay him one-third of their profits on the paving contract. They set up the special plea that the contract was void because it was an agreement to pay for lobby services, and in support of this plea they were obliged, of course, to represent that Parsons, who was the principal agent of Chittenden, and General Garfield, who was retained by Parsons for a short time as his counsel, were employed to influence members of Congress. Chittenden demurred to this plea; that is, he urged that, even if the facts were as the defendants alleged, the defense was not good in law. The issue being on this point alone, Judge Farwell overruled the demurrer; in other words, to cite the language of 'an able lawyer of Chicago,' whose letter was printed in the *World* on the 26th inst., 'The special pleas were held good, *if the facts were as therein stated.'* '

The plea set up Chittenden's letters to De Golyer & McClelland showing how the contract was obtained, and one of those letters detailed the retention of Garfield, not as a lawyer, but as chairman of the committee on appropriations, a simple word from whom would be a command to Shepherd. Judge Farwell, of the circuit court of Cook county, Illinois, held as stated. The pleas were good, 'if the facts were as therein stated.' Were the facts as therein stated the next proceedings in the case might disclose, but there were no further proceedings, for Chittenden, confronted by his own letters, went no further."

EXTRAVAGANCE.

The "extravagance" of the Republican party is certainly beyond anything of the kind known in the history of American politics. In proof of which the following data of facts is ample.

The expenses of the government of the United States, for the seventy-three years closing with 1861, were $1,506,726,151. This, of course, was under Federalist, Whig and Democratic administration. Compare with this the expenses of running the government for the *ten* years from 1866 to 1876, under Republican administration! The *ordinary* expenses of the government for the ten years immediately succeeding the war were $1,528,-

917,137.80, or $22,190,986.80 more for these ten years than for the seventy-three years preceding the war. It is true that there was a great increase in population, but as will be seen by the per capita expense, there was not sufficient increase of population to give any color of warrant for such increase of expense as this.

The ten years immediately preceding the war cost $572,872,260 — this under Democratic rule — only a little over one third of what it cost the ten years succeeding the war under Republican rule.

The average expense, per annum, during these two periods was, Democratic $57,287,216, while the Republican average was $150,672,614. But as these periods represented something of a difference in population, in order to be entirely fair we will estimate the per capita expense of running the government, per annum. We find it to have been, Democratic $18.26; Republican $39.65.

REBEL CLAIMS AND PENSIONS.

The following extract from the Chicago *Times* will, no doubt, be a great source of comfort to the timid who regard the election of Hancock as inevitable and are oppressed with consequent fear for the safety of the Republic:

" Judge Edmonds is a profound lawyer, an able

statesman, and all that, but he seems not to be acquainted with that part of the consititution of the United States of America which declares: 'But neither the United States nor any State shall assume or pay any debt or obligation incurred in aid of insurrection or rebellion against the United States, or any claim for loss or emancipation of any slaves, but all such debts, obligations and claims shall be held null and void.' His ignorance of this fundametal law is assumed from his assertion in a recent speech that 'the North would be taxed to pay rebel claims and pensions.'"

It is presumed, of course, that every American citizen who knows enough to vote intelligently, understands that before any "rebel claims" could possibly be paid it would be necessary to amend the constitution, and that this could only be done with the ratification of three-fourths of all the voters of the United States. It will, therefore, be seen that even were the late Confederates and the Democrats disposed to do it, they would be powerless.

The author desires to apologize for the seeming necessity of a notice of this most feeble resort of Republicans. It seems incredible that a gentleman of the former high position of Mr. Edmonds could stoop to such a pitiably silly position.

In regard to the other sole remaining "argument"

that lingers around the conventional sneer at the "Solid South," suppose the question were asked who made the south "Solid?" Who indeed but the very men now driven to the extremity of sneers. And how? Hell itself would blush in the presence of a full answer to this question, and there is not an intelligent Republican politician in America but who knows it. Such a system of legislation and tyranny would have smirched the reign of Caligula. And who of all those people have you taken to your bosoms — rewarded with political preferment? Longstreet who caused more loyal blood to drench the southern soil than any general of the Confederate armies! The butcher of Fort Pillow — his name is too infamous to repeat. And you would have taken the monster of Andersonville to the same loving embrace, aye, though the bony fingers of his murdered dead had clutched his throat to tear him from you, you had beat them off to revel in his loathsomest caresses, if by so doing you could have made the south "Solid" for the Republican party, *and you know it.*

Oh, gentlemen! make at least a *showing* of decency in this canvas.

THE LETTER OF JUDGE DAVIS.

Judge David Davis, than whom there is not an abler jurist, a purer statesman, or a more estimable gentleman—who, through a long and eventful career, has been admired for his noble, dignified and independent bearing on all things, writes as follows:

BLOOMINGTON, ILL., August 4, 1880.

My dear Sir: The training and the habits of my life naturally lead me to prefer civilians to soldiers for the great civil trust. But, as parties are organized, voters must choose between the candidates they present, or stand aloof, indifferent or neutral, which no good citizen ought to do at a presidential election.

I have no hesitation in supporting Gen. Hancock, for the best of all reasons, to my mind, because his election will put an end to sectional strife and to sectional parties, and will revive a patriotic sentiment all over the land, which political leaders and factions, for sinister ends, have sought to prevent. There can be no permanent prosperity without pacification.

Great as were the achievements of Gen. Hancock in war, his conduct in peace, when in command of Louisiana and Texas, in 1861, was still greater, and justly commends him to the confidence of the country.

That was a time when passion ruled in the public councils, and military power was exerted to silence civil authority. The temptation was strong to sail with the rushing current, for an inflamed partisan opinion was too ready to condone excesses and to applaud oppression.

Gen. Hancock's order No. 40, in assuming charge of the Fifth military district, announced: "The right of trial by jury, the habeas corpus, the liberty of the press, the freedom of speech, the natural rights of persons, and the rights of property must be respected."

These principles are the basis of free government, and the proclamation of them by Gen. Hancock stands out in striking contrast with the action of his superior, who soon after rebuked and drove him from that command for uttering sentiments worthy of all honor.

The soldier clothed with extraordinary power voluntarily uncovered before the civil authority, sheathed his sword, testified his fidelity to the constitution, and set an example of obedience to law which will pass into history as his proudest claim to distinction.

The man who, in the midst of the excitements of that stormy period, was cool enough to see his duty clearly, and courageous enough to execute it firmly, may well be trusted in any crisis.

His letter to Gen. Sherman, recently brought to light, lifts Gen. Hancock far above the past appreciation of his civil ability. It marks him as one of the wisest of his time, with a statesman's grasp of mind, and with the integrity of a patriot whom no sense of expediency could swerve from his honest convictions.

Long and unchecked possession of power by any party leads to extravagance, corruption, and loose practices. After twenty years of domination by the republicans, chronic abuses have become fastened on the public service, like barnacles on the bottom of a stranded ship.

There is no hope of reform by leaders who have created a system of maladministration, and who are interested in perpetuating its evils. Nothing short of the sternest remedy gives any promise of effective reform, and the first step toward it is in a change of rulers. The government must be got out of the ruts in which it has too long been run. New blood must be infused into the management of public affairs before relief can be expected.

The people demand change, and, being in earnest, they are likely to be gratified.

Very sincerely,

DAVID DAVIS.

James E. Harvey, Esq., Washington City."

HANCOCK AT NEW ORLEANS.

"The laws, they must be enforced — but the military shall remain in strict subordination to civil authority."

"The right of trial by jury, as maintained by our fathers, shall remain inviolate."

"The writ of habeas corpus, it must and shall be preserved in all its purity."

"Free speech and free press shall not be disturbed." —*General Hancock, at New Orleans.*

www.ingramcontent.com/pod-product-compliance
Lightning Source LLC
Chambersburg PA
CBHW031243260626

47169CB00007B/2433